THE BROTHEL NEXT DOOR

Enfys Eostre is the author of *The Brothel Next Door*, her debut novel. A woman from the strange side of the moon, Enfys lives her life in the United Kingdom. When she's not writing, she enjoys travelling and learning. You can catch up with her on her writer's Instagram page:
www.instagram.com/EnfysEostre

THE BROTHEL NEXT DOOR

Enfys Eostre

FIRST EDITION

Chapter One

It was a bright July Saturday in the bustling coastal town of Flemington in the southeast coast of England. The sun shone down upon the citizens of this seaside township. There were many among the denizens who soaked up the seemingly rare occurrence of sunshine on their shores. Among the excited tourists were busy residents who went about their regular lives of work and school. Within this, two university students huddled together in a moving van. The duo were uncomfortably sweaty but knew they had an important task ahead.

"Sarah-Jane, couldn't you have hired out a van with working air conditioning?" The passenger complained. Sarah-Jane faced her for a brief moment before refocusing her eye on the road ahead.

"I'll make sure we get a refund Kizzie," Sarah-Jane answered. Her long flowing hair was tied back in a sensible ponytail whilst her fringe was kept back by a hairband. Kizzie shifted uncomfortably in her seat. Her vest was slowly being drenched in sweat. Sarah-Jane flickered her eye towards Kizzie's vest. She smirked as she faced the road once more.

"Having said that if I get you hot enough now it'll make Diana's night easier," Sarah-Jane retorted.

"You're not funny." Kizzie responded. She was trying her best to repress a smile that was making its way across her face.

"Are you smiling because I'm right or because I'm funny?" Sarah-Jane cheekily asked. A silence fell upon the van.

"Both?" Kizzie tisked. The women giggled quietly as they continued their journey.

The moving van turned into a quiet road on the outskirts of town and stopped outside a semi-detached house. A man and a woman are waiting for them outside of the house they stopped by. Kizzie and Sarah-Jane took their seatbelts off and quickly sprung out of the van. They approached the man and woman who seemed somewhat relieved to see them.

"I bring you the last of our things," Sarah-Jane announced triumphantly. Kizzie approached the woman and tried to hug her but was stopped.

"Kizzie, you're sweaty as hell." The woman complained.

"So are you Diana," Kizzie replied as she kissed her on the cheek.

"I didn't think that would be a problem for you two normally," Sarah-Jane chimed in, "Wouldn't you think so Reuben?" Reuben, the man, rolled his eyes.

"Wrong context," he quipped, "There's not enough velour." Kizzie and Diana faced them with some indignation.

"Before we reveal our entire sex lives to our new neighbours, why don't we get the things out of the van?" Diana and Kizzie walked straight to the back of the van. Reuben nudged Sarah-Jane.

"Have you heard back from the office job?" Reuben asked.

"No," Sarah-Jane responded, "They did say it could be a couple of weeks until successful candidates are contacted. I need to wait another week before my rejection is confirmed."

"What are you going to do?"

"I've got that month-long temp job coming up. That'll tide me over for now." Reuben and Sarah-Jane got to the back of the van and devoted their energy to lifting the boxes into their new home.

The night descended upon the coastal skies. A darkness fell on the township as most residents wound down for the night. The van had long been emptied. Reuben, Kizzie, Diana and Sarah-Jane sat in a circle on the living room floor, surrounded by packed boxes. A half drunk bottle of rosé wine accompanied two other bottles sat in the centre of their circle. Their exhaustion was relieved by alcohol and friendly conversation.

"I don't know about you," Reuben started, "but I'm not fucking around this year. No fuck boys this year for me. I've got to knuckle down on my studies."

"You said that last year." Kizzie responded.

"Come to think of it," Diana added, "You said something along those lines when we met during our first Freshers Week." Reuben sipped his drink and thought for a moment.

"Shit," he realised, "I've become a gay cliche."

"Embrace promiscuity if that's what you want to do," Sarah-Jane said as she comforted him, "As long as you're not misleading anyone and it's legal, who cares?"

"Tonight, the voice of no bullshit reasoning will be played by Sarah-Jane Weston." Diana laughed as she jokingly raised her glass. Sarah-Jane gulped the remainder of her drink.

"Society can get over itself," Sarah-Jane continued, "Whatever happens between consenting adults is their fucking business. Thank you for coming to my TED talk."

"That's a TED talk I'd want to watch live," said Kizzie.

"I may have to wait until I finish my degree," Sarah-Jane conceded, "I don't want Becky Matthews' God squad on my back."

"I can divert them by snogging some fit man," Reuben jokingly suggested.

"At the same time Kizzie and I can start scissoring each other," Diana continued, "They'd be so enraged they'd totally forget about your TED talk." Sarah-Jane giggled with some delight.

"I should just get Luuk over and -" Sarah-Jane started. She was interrupted by a message alert on her phone. A silence fell among the group.

"Speak of the devil: it's Luuk," Sarah-Jane explained, "He wants to Skype me. I'll be back later." She got up from the floor and carefully tiptoed around her friends and the alcohol.

"Tell him to get his gorgeous Dutch arse back to the UK." Reuben exclaimed drunkenly. Sarah-Jane smiled as she closed the door behind her.

"How was your move?" A soft yet deep voice bristled from the phone Sarah-Jane was holding. Luuk appeared on the screen a second later. His blue eyes were offset with his tidy blonde hair. Sarah-Jane smiled when she saw his face.

"It was good," she answered, "I haven't started unpacking yet. All I have is a sleeping bag and my pillow."

"Why didn't you unpack?"

"Reuben insisted on a wine session. It was too appealing to resist after a day stuck in a crappy van."

"That sounds fair," Luuk giggled, "I hope the hangover isn't too bad."

"I'll have some water before bed," Sarah-Jane assured him. Luuk started to grin. His expression is noticed by Sarah-Jane.

"What?" she asked.

"Was the van too hot for you?" Luuk asked. Sarah-Jane was a little thrown off by a question with a seemingly obvious answer.

"Boiling" she responded.

"Wouldn't it be better if you could take your clothes off?" Luuk smirked as the realisation hit Sarah-Jane's face. She smirked.

"Yeah," she answered as she relaxed a little, "Better still if you could take my clothes off for me." She bit her lip a little.

"Mm. I'd come into the back of the van when you got the last box," Luuk started as he unzipped his jeans, "slip off your ondergoed and play with you." He unbuttoned his jeans. A noticeable bulge pressed against his cotton boxers. Sarah-Jane placed her free hand towards her vagina. She felt a flush of excited heat wash over her as she began to feel tantalised. Her index finger tentatively moved towards her clitoris.

"Did you close the door?" she asked in a soft, low tone.

"Maybe I did," Luuk purred, "It may be a little open."

"I hope we don't get caught. The risk," she panted as her finger edged close, "It turns me on as I touch your dick." Luuk slipped his hand down his boxers. He started to stroke his sizable, erect penis. Sarah-Jane watched with hungry anticipation as she began to tenderly stroke her clitoris. She inhaled as the overwhelming feeling of arousal started to take her over the more she played with herself.

"Like that," she panted as she watched Luuk masturbate. The more she watched, the more she wanted to touch him. Luuk smiled with satisfaction watching Sarah-Jane start to moan.

"It wouldn't be long until I was inside of you," Luuk whispered, "I'd have you against the wall with your legs wrapped around me, clinging to me as I fuck you harder and harder." Sarah-Jane felt her vagina pulsate as she slipped her fingers inside herself. She began to finger herself. She was edging close to orgasm. She faced Luuk who was pleasuring himself with delight. She could sense his concupiscence.

"You want me, don't you?" she asked, "I'm so wet. You want to fuck me right now."

"Yes"

"You want to make me scream. You want me to cling to you as I come on you again, and again, and again."

Sarah-Jane fingered herself faster and faster as she got closer and closer to coming.

"I'd let you," she continued, "and I'd beg you to keep fucking me. I can't get enough." As she spoke she orgasmed. She could barely keep her moans down as her body rushed with pleasure. Seeing her like this made Luuk more excited.

"Yes," he moaned, "I want you to come for me." At that, he let out an almighty groan as he climaxed. Sarah-Jane kept coming as she saw Luuk finish. She stopped. Her arm fell out of exhaustion. She tried to catch her breath. She turned to see Luuk who grabbed some tissue.

"Do you not have any?" He asked. She smiled at him.

"I have an ensuite now," she replied, "I'm going to sort myself out. I'll sleep soundly tonight." She winked at him. He smiled.

"One day I can do that for real." Luuk said wistfully.

"I'm sure you can fit me in between work and the metamour," Sarah-Jane responded cheekily, "In the meantime? Goodnight."

"Goodnight, Sarah-Jane."

Sarah-Jane hung up the phone. She hoisted herself up. She tread quietly to her new ensuite bathroom. As she went to grab some toilet roll, a slither of curtain was open. She heard the low murmur of a group of men talking. She approached the curtain. She saw a group of men leave the house together with their heads down. Sarah-Jane thought it seemed odd for a moment but moved away to clean herself.

Chapter Two

Twelve weeks rolled by so seamlessly for Sarah-Jane it seemed like no time at all. The only thing that caught her attention was the mysterious house attached to hers. On the outside there seemed to be nothing particularly extraordinary about the semi-detached house. It blended into every other house on the street, unassuming in its presentation. Sarah-Jane wasn't the sort of person to people-watch, but she couldn't help herself. She couldn't seem to work out who actually lived there nor why so many different men came in and out of it frequently. When she wasn't embarking on a futile job hunt or socialising, Sarah-Jane wondered about the house next door. That was until her final university year began classes.

It was a rainy Tuesday morning. Sarah-Jane rose from bed, knowing the day ahead. She charged down the stairs in her pyjamas, headed straight into the kitchen, went to the cupboard and grabbed a bowl. She got a hold of her cereal, poured some into her bowl and headed to the fridge. At this moment, Reuben came storming through the kitchen fully dressed in a stressed flurry.

"Where in the fucking fuck did I put my laptop?" Reuben fretted. Sarah-Jane got a hold of the semi-skimmed milk and turned to face Reuben.

"When did you last use it?" Sarah-Jane asked calmly.

"Last night. I was trying to find this Behavioural Finance book online before I tried the library."

"Did you leave it in the front room?" A moment of realisation came across Reuben's face as he bolted for the front room. Sarah-Jane shrugged to herself as she poured the milk into her cereal bowl. As she placed the milk back in the fridge, she started to hear the slight squeaks of moving springs above her. She was initially confused until she heard a very soft female moan in rhythm with the squeaking. Sarah-Jane started to eat her breakfast, unphased by the commotion. Reuben re-entered the room holding his laptop and a backpack. The squeaks and moans started to get faster and faster as time progressed.

"It's a good thing I found my laptop before they started," Reuben proclaimed as he placed his laptop in his backpack, "You can *really* hear them from the living room."

"I almost forgot about the joys of communal living during my placement last year," Sarah-Jane mused as she swallowed her mouthful of cereal, "Do they think we've already left?"

"Probably."

"We'll let them finish. They're not dicks to us when we bring people home."

"Don't ruin all my fun SJ!" Sarah-Jane glared at Reuben with a knowing look.

"Okay," she conceded, "ONE comment and that's your fill."

"Thank you, Mum."

"It better be good."

"Don't worry. I know what it'll be." Reuben smiled cheekily as he put his backpack on his back. Sarah-

Jane continued to eat her cereal. Reuben checked his watch. A few moments passed until the squeaking and moaning stopped. Reuben rushed towards the front door.

"3 more minutes and it would've been a new record!" Reuben gleefully yelled as he left the house. Sarah-Jane struggled not to choke as she giggled. She composed herself and kept eating her cereal. A dishevelled Diana came flying down the stairs. She is almost shocked to find Sarah-Jane finishing her bowl of cereal.

"Shit," Diana cursed, "I thought you'd be at university already."

"I told Reuben to leave it at one comment," Sarah-Jane tried to assure Diana, "He won't be a dick about it."

"He shouldn't be after the Copacabana party incident."

"Once I'm dressed I'll be heading to class. I've got Criminology of Borders today."

"Tell our dear Miss Matthews I said hi." Diana remarked sarcastically as she left the room.

"Gladly." Sarah-Jane smiled as she put the bowl and spoon in the sink.

Two hours had passed but Sarah-Jane was still smiling at the morning's happenings. Her hair flowed in the coastal wind as she approached the looming university building. She walked through the large doors and headed straight for her class. She approached her university classroom a few minutes early to her class. She advanced towards one of the desks in the middle of the classroom. She sat next to a short haired student.

"Hey Ehsan," Sarah-Jane greeted the student. They turned to face her and smiled.

"Hey stranger," Ehsan replied, "How was your summer?"

"Loud. I'm both happy and annoyed at communal living."

"Isn't that normal?"

"With my housemates? Absolutely. How was your placement?"

"Well -" Ehsan started. At that moment, the door flung open. A woman wearing a large pinafore dress with repressively tidy pigtails entered the room. She glared at Ehsan and Sarah-Jane. Sarah-Jane caught her eye. The woman approached her.

"If it isn't the-"

"Oh, look Ehsan: Becky Matthews is going to describe us in some offensive way because we belong to minority groups." Sarah-Jane interrupted.

"I have to wonder why she didn't just stay in Texas and get married like a good Christian girl." Ehsan mocked.

"She has to live out the Christian persecution complex a little longer on her own before finding a Billy Graham or Pat Robertson."

"You can't stand my righteous dedication to the Lord's work on Earth," Becky spluttered, "When this nation becomes a Christian nation again you sinners won't be laughing."

"If you're serving under God, why aren't you pregnant in the kitchen making your husband lunch?" Ehsan retorted.

"He has bigger plans for me!" Becky angrily responded.

"How convenient."

As Becky was about to answer, a man in his mid-forties stormed into the room wearing a sharp three-piece suit with his hair slicked back. He spots Becky with Ehsan and Sarah-Jane.

"Find a seat," the man barked at Becky, "I don't appreciate time wasters in my class." Becky scurried to a seat. As the lesson progressed, she kept glaring at Sarah-Jane and Ehsan. Sarah-Jane tried to concentrate on the lesson at hand whilst reminding herself mentally that she only had to deal with Becky Matthews for another year then she'd be free.

Six o'clock came around. Sarah-Jane entered her home after a full day of classes. As she closed the door, she realised how tense she felt. She kicked her shoes off and wondered quietly around the house to see if anyone else was around. The house was eerily silent.

"Reuben?" Sarah-Jane called out. She waited. She didn't get a response. She rushed to her bedroom and locked the door. She drew her curtains, jumped into bed and started loading her browser on her phone. She looked for a quick release to relieve her stress. She went on her favourite porn site: Straight, Sapphic and Something Else. She browsed until she found a video called 'Who's that Girl?"

"Perfect," Sarah-Jane muttered. She loaded the video and played it at low volume. As she followed the plot, she felt herself becoming more aroused. Her hand lay precariously above her vagina as she kept watching the pornographic film of two strangers hooking up. She was lost in her reverie as she imagined herself as one of the strangers. She got turned on by the fantasy of meeting an attractive stranger, only speaking for mere moments before rushing off to have sex hidden precariously away from oblivious passers-by. The anonymity was alluring and the risk of getting caught was simply an aphrodisiac. Sarah-Jane started to tenderly stroke her clitoris. She steadily got more enticed as she imagined herself as the woman in the porn getting her pussy licked by someone she met minutes ago. She started to lose herself in her

seductive dream as her body ached for orgasm.

Suddenly a loud, sharp bang echoed through

the house.

Chapter Three

Sarah-Jane snapped out of her dream and crashed back into reality. She was confused for a moment until she heard more heavy banging on her door.

"OPEN THE FUCKING DOOR!" A loud, male voice shouted. Sarah-Jane quickly composed herself. She stopped her porn, placed her phone in her pocket and rushed down the stairs. The banging continued.

"OPEN THE DOOR, COOKIE!" The man yelled again. This remark startled Sarah-Jane. She wasn't sure why this was going on. All she knew was she wanted this to stop so she could masturbate before her housemates came back.

"Who is this?" Sarah-Jane shouted back.

"I KNOW YOU'RE IN THERE, COOKIE."

"Who the fuck is Cookie?"

"YOU!"

"Evidently not," A tense pause filled the air for a brief moment. Sarah-Jane almost left her room to go down the stairs but decided against it.

"STOP PLAYING GAMES AND OPEN THE DOOR!" Sarah-Jane stayed put. She almost went for her phone when more slamming noises came from the front door. This jolted her into dropping her phone. The kicks became more aggressive until it broke open. An average sized man in his thirties was at her front door. He started raging around the house looking for someone. He kicked in all the doors downstairs in his hunt. Sarah-Jane was torn between calling the Police and remaining quiet. Her heart beat a million miles an hour as the man started coming up the stairs.

"Don't mess with me, bitch!" The man snarled as he came up the stairs. He tried to get into Sarah-Jane's room but couldn't. Before he could get in, a police car came barrelling to the house. Two police officers came rushing in. One police officer took him down, the other handcuffed him as he was read his rights. Both police officers held him until a police van rushed into view. Two other police officers came out of the van and took the man away.

"Miss, are you hurt?" The first police officer asked.

It was the following day. The autumn sun shone brightly across Flemington as the leaves turned from green to blood orange. Sarah-Jane sat alone in the living room in a blanket holding a cup of tea. She hadn't slept all night. She had been trying to process the events of the previous night. All she'd wanted to do was get off but instead she got terrorised by a man she'd never met before. Her silent contemplation was broken by a loud thud from downstairs. She immediately shot up and dropped her cup of tea.

"Shit!" Kizzie yelled. Sarah-Jane tried to pick up the pieces of her broken mug. Kizzie came down the stairs and saw Sarah-Jane trying to tidy up.

"Have you been to sleep yet?" Kizzie asked, concerned for Sarah-Jane.

"I couldn't sleep until the people came to fix the doors," Sarah-Jane explained. A silence fell between the pair. Sarah-Jane fiddled with her sleeve.

"They left a little while ago." Kizzie asked.

"I think I'm still a little bit wired from the incident" Sarah-Jane responded, "It all seemed to happen so fast."

"I get you. The police told us they reckon the man was searching for a sex worker he'd become infatuated with." Sarah-Jane raised her eyebrow.

"Did he even get the right street?" Sarah-Jane asked.

"The police don't know but I wouldn't put it past him trying to target that house next door." Kizzie confirmed. There was a knock at the door. This alarmed Sarah-Jane briefly before she heard:

"It's me," Diana shouted, "I haven't got a new key yet." Kizzie went to the new front door and let her in. They both came back to Sarah-Jane who'd calmed down.

"Have you been to sleep?" Diana asked Sarah-Jane, concerned. Sarah-Jane fiddled with a broken piece of her mug.

"You really need to get some sleep." Diana insisted, "You can't let this muck up your sleep cycle." At that moment, Sarah-Jane's phone started ringing. It was her mum.

"Mum,"

"Hi darling, I saw your text, are you okay?" Her mum fretted.

"She'll be fine" A male voice grumped in the background of Sarah-Jane mum's side of the call.

"Hi Bob," Sarah-Jane sighed.

"Sarah-Jane, sweetheart, we're going to pop by." Sarah-Jane's mum announced.

"Oh okay," Sarah-Jane yawned.

"We won't be long." Bob shouted from the other side of the phone.

"Mum, I love-" Sarah-Jane started before the phone hung up.

"I better get some coffee on," Sarah-Jane sighed, "Mum and Bob are on their way over."

Three hours later, Sarah-Jane sat in her living room across from her mum and Bob, her stepfather. She sat awkwardly with her cup of coffee. A bunch of flowers now sat on the living room table alongside a box of chocolates. An uncomfortable silence lasted between them.

"See? She's fine." Bob huffed.

"Darling, do you know why that man came to your home?" Sarah-Jane's mum asked, ignoring Bob's proclamation.

"I don't know," Sarah-Jane shyly, "But there's some talk that he was looking for an escort."

"Fucking prozzies," Bob mumbled. Sarah-Jane's eyes squinted slightly in disapproval.

"You can't call them that, Bob." Sarah-Jane argued.

"But they are fucking prozzies," Bob argued back, "They deserve what they get."

"No, they don't." Sarah-Jane exclaimed, "They deserve to be better protected."

"Don't make me laugh," Bob spat, "This is what you get by hanging about with those lesbos."

"Both of you, that's enough!" Sarah-Jane's mum shouted. A silence fell once again between the three of them.

"We better go," Bob announced, "I'm sure Sarah-Jane has lots of university work to catch up with." Sarah-Jane's mum looked weakly at Sarah-Jane then looked at Bob.

"Yes," Sarah-Jane's mum agreed. They all stood up. Sarah-Jane went to hug her mum, but Bob took her hand, and they left the living room, soon departing the house altogether.

"Love you too." Sarah-Jane scowled to herself. She took a chocolate from the chocolate box and ate it. As she finished, she heard a letter come through the letterbox. As she was about to get up, she heard Diana race down the stairs.

"I've got that, Weston!" Diana shouted as she raced to the front door. She came through to the living room with the letter in her hand.

"It's for you." Diana handed the letter to Sarah-Jane. The envelope was addressed to her by her first name without an address. Suspicious, Sarah-Jane carefully opened the letter. The letter was written neatly with a cursive hand. Sarah-Jane and Diana were perplexed for a moment.

"What does it say?" Diana asked.

"Sarah-Jane, I write to you with an apology," Sarah-Jane read, "The man who broke into your home last night wasn't trying to come for you. He had been harassing a friend of mine for some time in spite of a non-molestation order being active against him. I imagine in his blind rage he took it out on you."

"Shit."

"None of that justifies what he did to you last night."
Sarah-Jane continued, "I'm so sorry for what
happened to you. When you're feeling stronger please
feel free to come round for a cup of tea. Let me know
how I can help. Yours, the lady next door." Sarah-Jane
placed the letter next to her.

"That was unexpected," Diana commented, "Do you
reckon you'll go?"

"I need to think about it," Sarah-Jane conceded, "I
don't think this is a trap in any way."

"I agree. Wait until you've slept then consider it
properly."

"Good idea." Diana turned to leave.

Chapter Four

The next few days dragged on. She kept the letter in her underwear drawer, not wanting to deal with its contents for the time being. She distracted herself with university work. She consumed her thoughts with Land Law to help her through. By the fifth day she finally took the letter in her hand and read it again. She took it downstairs where her three housemates sat in the living room watching tv. As she approached the doorway all three turned to face her.

"How're you feeling?" Reuben asked as Sarah-Jane sat next to him on the sofa.

"A lot better than I have been thanks," Sarah-Jane responded.

"Are you still thinking about the letter?" Diana asked.

"Yeah. I've been thinking about it since I received it to be honest." Sarah-Jane responded. A pause filled the air.

"I'm going to go meet her tomorrow." Sarah-Jane confirmed.

"Are you sure?" Kizzie asked.

"Yeah. I'm sure. The fact we haven't been bombarded with letters suggests she isn't being nefarious." Sarah-Jane answered.

"Do you want one of us to come with you?" Kizzie asked.

"Yeah I can come as your gay bodyguard. I can throw glitter if they're homophobic." Reuben offered jokingly.

"I think I'll be okay to go alone," Sarah-Jane declined, "But perhaps we can agree on a codeword I can text if things go south?"

"If you text us something like 'I'm okay' every so often then we know you're alright," Diana suggested, "At least then if we don't hear from you at an interval we know we need to call the police."

"I best make sure I charge my phone then," Sarah-Jane accepted. Kizzie, Diana and Reuben smiled at her. Sarah-Jane felt touched by her friends' care for her but had a gut feeling that everything would turn out just fine.

Sarah-Jane approached the door of her next-door neighbours' house the following day. She tidied her hair and long, flowing dress. She was somewhat anxious until the door opened. A captivating, black-haired woman in her thirties was at the door dressed in a mermaid tail dress. Her make-up was striking, balanced between glam and goth.

"Yes?" the woman asked.

"I'm Sarah-Jane," Sarah-Jane answered, "I believe you wrote to me."

"Ah! I'm glad you came. Come into my living room for a drink." The woman invited Sarah-Jane in. Sarah-Jane was caught up in the juxtaposition of the normal looking interior of the house with the striking appearance of the woman at the door as they went into the living room. The living room was like any other run-of-the-mill living room, which seemed jarring with the glamorous appearance of the women

Sarah-Jane sat next to. A tray lay on the table with lemonade in a jug and two glasses.

"Lemonade?" The woman offered Sarah-Jane who nodded.

"I'm sorry," Sarah-Jane started as the lemonade was poured, "I didn't ask your name."

"Madame Beau," Madame Beau replied as she set the jug down, "My women call me Beau."

"Women?" There was a pause as Madame Beau handed Sarah-Jane a glass of lemonade.

"I have women work for me," Madame Beau answered, "One of them was the target of the man who broke into your home." Sarah-Jane took a sip of her lemonade. As she did, a knock on the door was heard. Madame Beau got up.

"Excuse me."

Sarah-Jane looked around the room as she waited for Madame Beau's return. Her stare turned to her lemonade glass. At that moment, a realisation clicked in her head. She took a sip of her lemonade as Madame Beau returned.

"I'm sorry about that," Madame Beau apologised.

"Madame Beau, are you running a brothel?" Sarah-Jane blurted. Madame Beau was taken aback but unoffended.

"What makes you say that?"

"I've noticed a lot of men coming and going from the house. I just found it a bit odd."

"You're sharp," Madame Beau complimented, "The last people who lived there didn't catch on once in five years."

"How does it work?" Sarah-Jane asked, curious. A part of her ached to know more about what was going on.

"The women who work for me run on a schedule based on what works best for them. I take a small percent of their earnings to keep things afloat. Otherwise, the money is theirs."

"How small are we talking?"

"10%."

"And where does that go?"

"Bills, clothes for the girls and a little salary for me."

"Any woman can sign up?"

"Why? Are you considering it?" This question

stunned Sarah-Jane for a moment as she considered her increased curiosity.

"Enough about me, my love," Madame Beau said, "What does a woman like you do for a living?"

"I'm a 4th year student. I'm studying Law and Criminology." Sarah-Jane answered.

"Let me guess: committed to the work rather than a person?"

"Sort of. I have a casual partner. Luuk. He's in the Netherlands. It's not anything that serious."

"You're young. It would be a shame not to explore yourself." Sarah-Jane bit her lip slightly as Madame Beau got a little closer to her. There was a palpable sexual tension between the two.

"If you ever need a job, come on by. There's an afternoon where we get to know what works for you, get your measurements, and sort a schedule. If you're still up for it then we can get you started." Madame Beau offered. Sarah-Jane sipped her lemonade.

"Could I see a different person each time or do I have to have regulars?" Sarah-Jane asked.

"You can see a different person if you like."

"I'd want to think about it first. How do I let you know?" Madame Beau slipped a piece of paper in Sarah-Jane's hand.

"Call me," Madame Beau responded with a wink. Sarah-Jane smiled as she took another sip of her lemonade.

Some hours rolled before Sarah-Jane came back home. She wandered through the silent house a moment until she realised she was alone. She rushed carefully up to her bedroom. She closed her door, drew her curtains and sat at her bed. She leaned back as she took her panties off. She spread her legs as she reached for herself. She started to play with herself as she thought about Madame Beau and her offer. She gently rubbed as she fantasised about meeting a stranger for sex. The caress of the unknown was tantalising for Sarah-Jane who was in the throes of sexual ecstasy as she imagined herself riding one stranger after another. She started to orgasm as the fantasies continued. She couldn't help but scream out in pleasure as her orgasm crashed to an end. Breathless and more relaxed, Sarah-Jane washed her hands and tidied herself up to go back downstairs.

She looked at the slip of paper she received from

Madame Beau. She left it on her bed and headed

downstairs.

Chapter Five

"So, what do you think?" Sarah-Jane asked her stunned housemates. Reuben, Kizzie and Diana's visible reaction was enough to make Sarah-Jane intensely anxious.

"Please say something." Sarah-Jane requested.

"You can't seriously be considering this." Diana started.

"It's nuts. You're a Law student. This is career suicide." Kizzie continued.

"Folks, it's not *that* odd surely? I mean brothels exist all over the place," Reuben argued, "Is it so odd that one happens to be next door to us?"

"That's not the problem Reuben," Diana rebutted, "It's the fact Sarah-Jane is considering putting herself at a needless risk by considering a profession like prostitution."

"Whatever happened to your 3rd wave pro-sex work feminism?" Reuben countered, "I thought you weren't against sex work."

"Yeah but," Diana struggled, "this is different."

"How?" Reuben asked. At that moment, Kizzie looked to where Sarah-Jane was standing only to see she was gone.

"Guys," Kizzie started.

"This is our friend. She's not someone who has no other options. It's not like she can't get a retail job."

"Guys," Kizzie repeated, slightly louder.

"Yes because retail jobs that allow for a final year university student are just lying around the place begging to be taken." Reuben sarcastically retorted.

"Be a grown up Reuben!" Diana snapped.

"Fucks sake," Kizzie muttered.

"I am. You're just trying to cover for being a hypo-" Reuben started.

"SHUT THE FUCK UP, BOTH OF YOU!" Kizzie yelled as she pointed to where Sarah-Jane was standing, "SJ has gone. I get your points, but she doesn't need either of you to make it a fight." Reuben and Diana sheepishly look at each other and Kizzie.

"So, you approve?" Sarah-Jane asks. She looks intently at Luuk across Skype, keen for some kind of validation.

"Do you need my approval?" Luuk responded.

"No but your support would be nice."

"Of course, I support you."

"You don't think it's career suicide?"

"No. As long as you keep it quiet and stop it when you're going for a job after graduation I don't see how it's a problem."

"Thank you," Sarah-Jane sighed in relief, "The others weren't exactly supportive. I thought they would've been."

"It's probably just a bit of a shock for them," Luuk theorised, "You British people are still far too hung up on that sort of thing."

"That's true," Sarah-Jane giggled softly.

"Give them a bit of time. They'll come around. They're decent people."

"Why are you so reasonable?"

"I'm a lawyer. Coming across as reasonable is a necessity." Sarah-Jane smiled fondly at Luuk.

"I wish I was there to give you a cuddle." Luuk responded.

"I wish you could be here to do that," Sarah-Jane added. They both sighed. The difficulties of their distance bubbled up in their hearts at that moment.

"We'll figure it out," Sarah-Jane said as she touched the screen, "We always do."

"Once you're settled into your university schedule, can we sort a visit?" Luuk proposed.

"I'd like that."

Two weeks passed by. Sarah-Jane was doing her make-up in her ensuite. She carefully brushed her lipstick upon her plump lips to finish her tidy, professional look. She examined her make-up to ensure all blemishes were covered. Satisfied, she grabbed her handbag that hung on her door handle. She headed down the stairs in anticipation of what the day would bring. As she went to the shoe rack, she bumped into Reuben.

"Today's the day?" Reuben asked awkwardly.

"Yeah," Sarah-Jane answered just as awkwardly. The awkward tension bothered both of them.

"I don't totally get it," Reuben admitted, "But I'm behind you 100%. It's your life and you have every right to make whatever damn decision you want."

"Thanks." Sarah-Jane hugged Reuben as the tension evaporated between them.

"I think Kizzie and Diana might need some more time." Reuben admitted.

"That's fair," Sarah-Jane answered, "It's probably just a bit of a shock."

"I best not delay you. Let me know how it goes." With that, Reuben headed into the living room. Sarah-Jane took a deep breath as she grabbed her slip-on black shoes. She slipped into her shoes, grabbed her front door and opened it. She slid out and shut the door quietly behind her. She skipped out and headed straight to Madame Beau's. She took a moment to compose herself before she knocked on the door. Madame Beau answered the door. Upon seeing Sarah-Jane, she smiled.

"Sarah-Jane," Madame Beau greeted her as she beckoned her in. Sarah-Jane went straight into the living room. Madame Beau shut the door behind her and drew the curtains.

"First things first, get down to your underwear so I can measure you." Madame Beau asked. Sarah-Jane unzipped her dress and stepped out of it. Madame Beau started to take her measurements.

"How're you feeling?" Madame Beau questioned Sarah-Jane.

"Okay," Sarah-Jane answered honestly, "Trying to find a job otherwise has been a nightmare."

"Glad I could help." Madame Beau continued to take Sarah-Jane's measurements. The sexual tension between the pair started to escalate as Madame Beau measured her chest.

"Do you have any hard limits?" Madame Beau asked as she wrote down Sarah-Jane's chest measurements.

"I'd rather not see the same client more than once unless otherwise specified. Shit, piss and blood play are a no no. Condoms are a must. I think I'm fine with everything else." Sarah-Jane replied.

"We can always go through a list to check," Madame Beau offered as she measured Sarah-Jane's legs, "Can I ask you a question?"

"Sure."

"Do you get off on stranger sex?"

Sarah-Jane paused before responding. "How can you tell?"

"Your insistence of only seeing a client once only is a give-away."

"I don't tend to talk about it."

"What is there to say? You enjoy stranger sex," Madame Beau said as she wrote down Sarah-Jane's leg measurements, "And this is a good way to explore that kink." Madame Beau stood up to face Sarah-Jane. The sexual tension between them started to boil as they remained close to each other.

"I'd like to know a bit more about your technique," Madame Beau asked in a sultry manner. Sarah-Jane was increasingly turned on.

"My technique?"

"You don't have to. I'm just curious." The sexual

tension between the pair became unbearable.

Madame Beau pulled Sarah-Jane into a passionate

kiss. Madame Beau cupped Sarah-Jane's breasts as

she sat on the living room sofa. Sarah-Jane unhooked

her bra. She knelt and reached for Madame Beau's top

and bra. She unhooked her bra. They looked briefly at

each other before Sarah-Jane started playing with

Madame Beau's breasts. She cupped her breasts

before licking her nipples. Madame Beau sank back

on to the sofa as she became increasingly aroused.

Before she knew it, Sarah-Jane slipped her hand down

Madame Beau's underwear. Sarah-Jane started to

play with Madame Beau's clitoris as she licked her

nipple. Madame Beau began to orgasm as Sarah-Jane

gradually increased her speed. As Madame Beau

orgasmed, Sarah-Jane became more and more aroused herself. Madame Beau spotted this.

"Wait," Madame Beau said as she stopped climaxing. Sarah-Jane stopped what she was doing.

"Are you okay?" Sarah-Jane asked.

"I'm great," Madame Beau replied as she stroked Sarah-Jane's cheek, "Lie down for me. You're dying to come." Sarah-Jane did as she was told and lay down on the floor. Madame Beau got up from the sofa. She took off Sarah-Jane's pants. She stroked Sarah-Jane's legs as she straddled her head.

"Hold tight." Madame Beau said as she positioned herself so her vagina was over Sarah-Jane's mouth. Madame Beau went down herself and began to perform cunnilingus on Sarah-Jane's wet pussy. Sarah-Jane started to groan in pleasure quietly as she started to eat out Madame Beau. As the 69 continued, both women kept on climaxing on each other as they both started using their fingers as well as their tongues on each other. As they reached climax, their free hand clung to each other as if their lives depended on it. Their orgasms start to slow down as they themselves start to slow their movements. Exhausted, Madame Beau rolled over onto the floor. Sarah-Jane sits up.

"Are there any tissues?" Sarah-Jane asked. She spotted a box of tissues. As she went to grab them, Madame Beau flung her hand and presented them to Sarah-Jane.

"Thanks," Sarah-Jane thanked as she started to tidy herself up. Madame Beau got up and started to compose herself.

"You recover quickly," Madame Beau noted.

"I always do," Sarah-Jane replied, "It's just a thing with me."

"That'll be useful when you start."

Chapter Six

A week went by. Sarah-Jane packed her make-up away into her wash bag, fully made up herself. She placed her wash bag in her handbag. She brushed her long hair, carefully preparing herself. As she grabbed her dress, she heard a knock on her door.

"SJ! Kizzie, Reuben and I are going to the cinema. Want to come?" Diana asked from behind the door.

"Sorry Diana," Sarah-Jane answered as she put her dress on, "I've got my first day of work."

"Oh." Diana paused. Sarah-Jane could tell there was an element of disappointment.

"After work, why don't we all get takeaway?" Sarah-Jane offered.

"I don't know if we have the money for it," Diana answered, "Thanks anyway." Diana left. Sarah-Jane opened the door to see Diana walk away. Feeling somewhat defeated, Sarah-Jane grabbed her handbag and headed downstairs. She grabbed a pair of her shoes, put them on and headed out the door without skipping a beat. As she walked towards Madame Beau's door, Sarah-Jane calmed her nerves by assuring herself that she was fine. Sarah-Jane knocked on Madame Beau's door.

"Well, if it isn't Ms Sarah-Jane," Madame Beau answered the door.

"I said I'd be here," Sarah-Jane quipped, "So where do you want me?"

Fifteen minutes passed. Sarah-Jane was now in a corset bridal dress with white kitten heels and a bridal veil. She read her given scenario: a naive, innocent, virginal woman about to get married whilst her client was to play the father of the groom who seduces her. A knock was heard at the door. She knew that now was show time.

"I'm ready." Sarah-Jane answered. At that moment, a man in his late thirties emerged from the door. He was dressed in a suit fit for a groom. His hair was gelled back whilst his beard was well groomed. His dark eyes lay on Sarah-Jane with desire.

"You know the scenario?" He asked sheepishly.

"Yeah," Sarah-Jane smiled, "Come in." The man came in. Sarah-Jane put her paper away, stood up and started the act.

"I'm so nervous, Sir." Sarah-Jane started.

"Hank, you can call me Hank," The man continued.

"Hank, I'm so happy to marry your son but I'm scared."

"Scared? Why?"

"I've never been with a man sexually. What if I'm no good?"

"Oh sweetheart," Hank soothed, "I'm sure you'll be great. I can help you." Hank approached Sarah-Jane with a look of determination in his eye and a smirk across his face. He held Sarah-Jane's hand and led her to the bed. They sat together.

"First," he instructed, "I'll show you what it should look like." Hank unzipped and took his trousers off. His erection was clear through his boxers as he removed them. He sat back on the bed again. Sarah-Jane, in her role, gasped.

"Hank, your penis is so big. How can something like that fit?"

"Touch it." He asked. Sarah-Jane tentatively touched his penis. Hank guided her hand as if to teach her how to jerk him off.

"Like that?" Sarah-Jane asked.

"Like that." Hank replied as he started to get increasingly turned on. He moaned softly as Sarah-Jane kept wanking him off.

"Are you turned on?" Hank asked. Sarah-Jane was starting to get turned on as well as she continued jerking off this stranger.

"Yes, Hank, sir," Sarah-Jane answered in character, "I feel all hot and tingly."

"You're doing such a good job," Hank murmured, "I should show you how you should be pleasured." With that, Hank pulled down Sarah-Jane's silken panties. He stared at her vagina for a moment before he spread her legs. He licked his lips and started to finger her wet pussy. Sarah-Jane was hit with a wave of pleasure. She started to groan as Hank got deeper. He was elated.

"You want me, don't you?"

"Yes Sir," Sarah-Jane panted as Hank's fingering got faster and faster. As he fingered her harder, Sarah-Jane struggled not to orgasm. She clung to the bed as Hank suddenly stopped. He looked at Sarah-Jane.

"My dear," he smirked, "Do you want me to be your first?"

"Yes Hank," she exclaimed, "I want you to be my first." With that, Hank got a condom out of his trouser pocket. He excitedly put the condom on, went back to Sarah-Jane and readied himself.

"I'll make you forget all about my son."

"I want you, Hank," Sarah-Jane exclaimed. Hank put his engorged penis into Sarah-Jane's warm and inviting vagina. He started to rock gently back and forth as he eased himself ever increasingly inside of her. Sarah-Jane groaned, surprised but pleased. His gentleness soon turned into uncontrolled passion as he continued to fuck her. Her corseted dress bunched up from the thrusts. The corset lowered down to reveal Sarah-Jane's breasts. Sarah-Jane felt the excitement build within her as this total stranger had sex with her. They were both getting exactly what they wanted and that made Sarah-Jane begin to climax. Her orgasms fuelled Hank even more.

"You wanted me. I knew it," Hank panted as he kept fucking her, "I knew you weren't so innocent." At that moment, Hank was overcome with his own orgasm. He suddenly stopped as his own orgasm crashed through his soul. He composed himself and started to retreat out of Sarah-Jane who went to grab some tissues.

Sarah-Jane sheepishly came through her front door some four hours later.

"Sarah-Jane, is that you?" A voice called out. Reuben came through the living room door with a takeaway menu.

"Yeah." Sarah-Jane replied, "Are you getting takeout?"

"Want to join in?" Reuben asked.

"Sure. I earned quite a bit today so it's on me."

"Sure? That's awesome!" Reuben excitedly went back into the living room. Sarah-Jane kicked off her shoes. She went into the living room. Kizzie and Diana were sitting cuddled together on the sofa.

"How was it?" Diana asked shyly.

"Honestly?" Sarah-Jane retorted, unsure.

"I know I haven't been the most supportive friend in the world about this," Diana explained, "I'm being a huge hypocrite by advocating for a woman's right to choose then getting arsey at you for your choice. If I'm going to get over myself I've got to understand."

"I appreciate it," Sarah-Jane answered, taken aback, "It was great. I get to explore my stranger sex kink and these people get to get off."

"What if they're not attractive to you?" Kizzie asked.

"None of them were particularly attractive. They were just strangers."

"You do use a condom, right?"

"Duh. I'm not risking shit from someone I can't trace."

"This talk is great," Reuben interjected, holding the takeout menu in the air, "But I'm fucking starving and will eat you lot if we don't get takeout." As

Kizzie and Reuben read through the menu, Diana rushed to Sarah-Jane and hugged her.

"I'm sorry." Diana apologised.

"Thank you." Sarah-Jane accepted. They broke away and gathered around the takeout menu with Reuben and Kizzie.

Chapter Seven

The following week rolled around: Reading week. A week off for university students to study. For Sarah-Jane it was a good opportunity to prop up her income in between book readings. She went next door on Monday, fully prepared for the week ahead. As she came through the door, she eagerly awaited what was ahead of her.

"Madame Beau, what's on the table for me?" Sarah-Jane asked as she spotted Madame Beau.

"Your first client of the day is a Princess/Peasant scenario," Madame Beau answered, "It'll be easy - this guy has a major fetish for pleasing other people."

"Brilliant."

"Your costume is in your usual bedroom. He's not due for another 30 minutes so you've got time to get into your costume."

"Perfect. Thanks Madame."

"I won't be in when you finish so can you pick up your pay for today tomorrow?"

"Of course," Sarah-Jane responded. Sarah-Jane headed upstairs without a moment's pause.

30 minutes went by. Sarah-Jane was dressed in a corset pink dress adjourned with fake jewels and lace. She admired herself as she put on the diamante earrings. She tidied up her hair as she heard the door knock tentatively.

"Come in," she called. At that moment, a nervous looking man came in. Short, balding and round he approached Sarah-Jane. She sat on her chair. He bowed and knelt to the floor.

"Your Royal Highness, I have nothing to offer," he started, "I'm a mere subject. I am -"

"Did I ask for your life story, peasant?" Sarah-Jane retorted.

"No, ma'am," he said as he put his hands on the floor. He gently caressed her feet, "I only ask that I may pleasure your Royal Highness." Sarah-Jane looked upon the man. She didn't seem to expect much but the excitement she felt to have sex with someone she didn't know kept her in the moment.

"Very well. You may pleasure your Princess." Sarah-Jane commanded. The man smiled as she parted her legs. She lifted her skirt up to reveal her inviting pussy. He looked up at her, grinning.

"Thank you, your Royal Highness." He thanked her as he drew his face closer to Sarah-Jane's vagina. He softly brushed his fingers against her aching clitoris. She started to pant softly as he gently touched her. Without warning he started to aggressively lick her out. This took Sarah-Jane aback as he clung to the chair. Before she knew it she was panting with lust as he continued to eat her out. Sarah-Jane couldn't maintain any sort of composure, especially when she felt his fingers slide in and out of her. She clung on to the chair as her orgasm crescendoed over her. At that moment, the man emerged from under her skirt.

"Is my Princess pleased?" The man asked. Sarah-Jane composed herself and sat up straight.

"Yes but your Princess wants more." Sarah-Jane responded. She got up, approached the bed and sat with her legs wide apart. Her dress was parted appropriately. She dirtily smirked at the man as his boner became obvious through his trousers. He gulped.

"Your Highness," he sputtered, "It would be my pleasure." He quickly shuffled into his pockets and drew out a condom. He removed his trousers and underwear. As he put his condom on, Sarah-Jane started to tease him by playing with herself.

"Oh peasant," she cooed, "I'm waiting." The man carefully put his condom on and drew in on Sarah-Jane. He excitedly put his penis inside of her vagina. He rocked steadily and kept his eye on Sarah-Jane who started to softly moan. She kept rubbing her clitoris as he fucked her. The dress crumbled up towards Sarah-Jane's chest. Another orgasm began to build within Sarah-Jane. As the orgasm built, she rubbed harder and faster. She felt herself start to orgasm when, out of nowhere, the man groaned loudly as he came inside of her. He held onto the bed, exhausted. Sarah-Jane's chances of an orgasm again melted away as the man got out of her.

"I'm sorry," the man apologised, "It happens."

"You were fine," Sarah-Jane assured him.

"Thanks."

Later that night, Sarah-Jane was sitting on her bed with her laptop left running. She was reading a legal textbook. The next thing she knew, her laptop started ringing. It was Luuk. Sarah-Jane put away her textbook and answered the call.

"Hello," Sarah-Jane greeted, "I thought you were -"

"At Zara's parents' house? I am. I just told them I had to check in with work," Luuk answered.

"Sneaky bastard." Sarah-Jane smiled and blushed slightly.

"You think it's cute?"

"A little."

"That's cute," Luuk remarked, "How was your work today?"

"It was quite fun. I got to be a Princess whose peasant was into pleasuring her."

"That must've been a nice change."

"Yeah and now I'm just plunging into Land Law." Sarah-Jane sighed, "How is it at Zara's parents?"

"They're lovely but they don't have the best concept of personal space."

"My evil scheme of making Land Law sound dirty wouldn't be a good idea right now?"

"They're quite conservative people. We haven't even told them about our non-monogamy."

"I best behave then."

"You better do it." At that moment, a knock on Sarah-Jane's bedroom door was heard.

"Bitch get decent and come downstairs," Reuben shouted from the other side, "I'm making cocktails."

"In a minute!" Sarah-Jane responded.

"I better not stick around for long, but I do want to sort a trip out soon. Maybe on our next call?" Luuk asked.

"Sounds good," Sarah-Jane responded.

"Miss you." This admission threw Sarah-Jane aback a little.

"I miss you too." She sweetly replied.

"He told you he missed you?" Reuben asked in the kitchen as he prepared a pitcher of Cosmopolitan. A pitcher of Sex On The Beach was already sitting waiting to be drunk.

"Yeah," Sarah-Jane replied.

"Did you say it back?"

"Yeah."

"Oh babe, you two are catching feelings." Reuben teased.

"It's not a big deal. Casual partners can miss each other, right?"

"When they're catching feelings for each other they can."

"I knew confiding in you was a bad idea."

"I'm your gay bestie!"

"*One* of my gay besties."

"The others don't exist in my cinematic universe." Reuben and Sarah-Jane laughed together. At that moment Diana and Kizzie entered the kitchen.

"What's the occasion?" Diana asked, pointing at Reuben's cocktail preparation.

"Reuben is bored during Reading week." Sarah-Jane answered.

"None of you appreciate how horrifyingly dull Behavioural Finance is," Reuben tisked as he continued making.

"Just hearing you say, 'Behavioural Finance' makes me want to drink my brains out." Kizzie laughed.

"So how was work today, Sarah-Jane?" Diana asked.

"I did Princess roleplay. It was interesting," Sarah-Jane answered, "The guy had a giving pleasure fetish which I didn't hate."

"I've got to say, you seem a bit happier at the moment." Kizzie noted.

"I am," Sarah-Jane admitted, "The money is pretty good and it's on my own terms. I can't fault it." At that moment, Reuben finished the cocktail and got glasses from out of the cupboard.

"Bitch faces, it's time for drinks," Reuben declared.

The following day dawned in the town of Flemington. Sarah-Jane arose from her bed with a lingering hangover.

"Fucking Reuben," she muttered as she dragged herself out of bed. She turned to her alarm clock. It was 10:30am. She sighed.

"At least I have an hour for breakfast." Sarah-Jane thought. She grabbed a long, flowing dress from her wardrobe. She placed it on the bed as she tried to find her underwear. At that, Sarah-Jane's mobile started ringing. She grabbed it quickly.

"Hello?"

"Sarah-Jane, good time?" Madame Beau spoke over the phone.

"What's up Beau?"

"One of the other girls has come down with a bug. She has an appointment waiting. Can you make it over?"

"Sure," Sarah-Jane answered as she got her underpants on, "I just need to finish getting dressed and I'll be over in a few." As she said that she grimaced. Breakfast would have to come later.

"You're a star," Madame Beau said, "It's a Vampire/Vampire Slayer role play. You're the Slayer. The guy is going to overpower you and have his way. The safe word is his name: Adam".

"Thanks for the brief."

"I have some lubricant if you need it. He's not much for foreplay."

"Thanks Madame. I'll be there in a few minutes." Sarah-Jane hung up. She hurriedly put her bra on, grabbed her dress, slung it on and ran downstairs. She grabbed her shoes from the shoe rack in the hallway. At that moment, Kizzie came stumbling through, hungover.

"How are *you* not hungover?" Kizzie asked.

"Trust me: I am. I just had a call from work. I've got to cover a girl."

"You make it sound so casual."

"I would get into this but," Sarah-Jane said as she got her shoes on, "I really don't have time. At that moment she ran out of the door.

Twenty minutes later, Sarah-Jane was in her usual room at Madame Beau's. She was now dressed in a black strapless mini dress and crotchless panties with a stake in her hand. She did up her knee-high boots as the door knocked. Sarah-Jane grabbed her lubricant sachet. She ripped it open and lubricated her pussy.

"Come in." At that moment, Adam entered. He was a young man wearing a black shirt with black jeans, a long leather jacket and black shoes.

"Slayer." He scowled as he looked up and down at Sarah-Jane. She raised her stake. He laughed. She went for him, but he grabbed her stake arm. He carefully twisted her arm back as he grabbed her other arm.

"You can't escape me," Adam growled as he pushed Sarah-Jane onto the bed. He unzipped his trousers to reveal his throbbing erection. He looked through his pockets but couldn't find what he was looking for.

"I'm sorry," Adam apologised as he broke character, "Do you have a condom? I must've left mine at home."

"Oh sure," Sarah-Jane replied. She went to her drawer and handed him a condom. She took her position back on to the bed as he placed the condom on his member. He reverted back into character.

"You're mine, Slayer." He snarled as he moved over to Sarah-Jane. He leaned on top of her. He maintained eye contact as he placed his penis inside of her. She gasped.

"You want me. Admit it." He smirked.

"I want you. I know that now." She replied. He pushed himself deep inside of her. The sudden thrust caused a little pain within Sarah-Jane, softened only by the gel lubricant. She whimpered slightly.

"C'mon Slayer, it'll be fun." Adam gnarled. He began to slip his engorged member back and forth violently. Sarah-Jane tensed slightly at the sudden pain but ran with it. She started to slip a hand towards her crotch.

"You're so ferocious," Sarah-Jane panted, "I can't control myself." Her hand reached her clitoris, and she began to gently massage her clitoris. As she caressed herself, she felt the familiar burgeoning build-up of an orgasm flow through her. The feeling overtook her senses as she groaned. Her free hand clutched the bed sheets.

"Oh God yes." She moaned. This encouraged Adam who kept thrusting back and forth, faster and faster. The more he continued, the bigger the build-up became until the wave of an intense orgasm hit Sarah-Jane like water crashing on the beach. As she came Adam smirked.

"You're mine, Slayer." he panted. At that moment, he went for Sarah-Jane's shoulder and bit down hard. This turned Sarah-Jane on more as she rubbed herself faster and faster. The moment climaxed as the man raised his head from Sarah-Jane's shoulder.

"Score!" Adam screamed as he orgasmed into Sarah-Jane. Exhausted, Adam collapsed on top of Sarah-Jane who removed her hand from herself. A moment passed before Adam started removing himself from inside her. As he looked down at her, his face scrunched up.

"Uh, I might've been a bit too rough," Adam remarked, "There's blood here." Sarah-Jane, alerted, sat straight up. She looked down and realised a small puddle of blood was forming on the white sheet.

"Can you do me a favour? Before you go, ask Madame Beau to bring a sanitary pad?"

"Of course," Adam fumbled awkwardly as he got himself dressed, "You were great."

"Thanks."

"Can I see you again?"

"I'm sorry, no. I have a strict once-only policy."

"Oh."

Chapter Eight

A week slipped by. Adam was walking along the road towards the University of Flemington's campus. In contrast to last week's outfit, he wore a buttoned-up shirt, trousers and a tie. He entered the university apprehensive. He rushed through the corridors to enter a room with the sign "Christian Conservative meeting" scribbled across it. He cleared his throat before he knocked on the door.

"Come in!" A female voice shouted. Adam opened the door. He came into the room to find Becky sitting alone, tapping her foot impatiently.

"You're early, Adam," she snapped.

"Is anyone else here yet, Becky?" Adam asked desperately.

"No. Why?"

"I needed to talk to you. I didn't know who else to turn to." Adam grabbed the seat next to Becky.

"I've sinned. I gave into my worst impulses, and I sinned. I can't turn to anyone else." Becky leaned in closer.

"There are many passages to forgiveness in the eyes of the Lord. The first step is to admit our sins. What did you do?"

Adam hesitated.

"I went to a local brothel and had sex with a prostitute." Adam began to cry. Becky went to pat his back but stopped herself as if to stop herself getting dirty.

"That's quite a sin," she condescendingly chimed,

"But you're not lost. Not yet. Where is this brothel?"

"I can't tell," Adam spluttered, "I'm the one who

sinned."

"They're living in eternal sin Adam," Becky chided,

"The only way to save them from themselves is to tell

me where it is so we can stop their evil practice."

Adam grabbed a tissue from his trouser pocket and

blew his nose. He turned to Becky whose smile was

almost as plastic as the chair she sat on.

"What if they don't need saving? Jesus hung out with

prostitutes in the Bible."

"Adam, you're a good Christian man. I would hate

for this to get out." Adam looked down at the floor as

he contemplated Becky's words. He looked back at

her.

"Eddington Road. 26 Eddington Road." Adam sighed. Becky patted his back.

"You did the right thing, friend." she comforted as she grinned.

That same night, Sarah-Jane was on a Skype call to Luuk. She was dressed in a dressing gown and pyjamas.

"Are you able to get back to work?" Luuk asked.

"I should be able to by the end of the week," Sarah-Jane replied, "I would go back tomorrow but I've got to make a move on my dissertation."

"Good idea to get that started early. I remember my dissertation. I rushed it in a haze."

"I'm desperate to get as good a grade as possible. This means I need to buckle down."

"Don't buckle too hard," Luuk teased, "I'd like to see some semblance of you." Sarah-Jane smiled.

"Speaking of seeing, I was thinking about what you said in our last Skype call. What about a Christmas trip? I'm not saying Christmas per se but maybe around then?"

"Well, that's a bit of a way away." He hesitated.

Sarah-Jane's heart sank. "It doesn't have to be Christmas. Maybe just December generally?" She tried.

"I don't know." He hesitated again. Sarah-Jane sensed a panic in his answer and decided to back off.

"Forget it." An awkward silence hung in the air. Sarah-Jane fiddled with her dressing gown cord.

"Let's not argue," Luuk panicked, "Why don't we do something fun? I can pretend to be a strange man at a bar."

"I'm not in the mood. I'm feeling a bit wiped," Sarah-Jane replied, "I'm going to go to bed."

"Okay. Goodnight."

"Goodnight." Sarah-Jane hung up. Feeling defeated, she climbed into bed.

A few days flew past. Sarah-Jane was back happily at work. She was preparing for her next client by getting changed into a slutty student outfit. Her shirt fit tightly across her breasts as her skirt rode so high up her, her lack of underwear was visible. She heard a knock on the door.

"Come in." She shouted. She heard the door nervously open. A middle-aged man came through the door dressed in a tweed suit. He closed the door behind him.

"I've never done this before." The man admitted.

"Don't worry Sir," Sarah-Jane assured, "It's very easy. We can just go into the roleplay and see how it goes. Do you have a condom?"

"Yeah I do."

"Then we're already off to a good -"

At that moment, a loud bang could be heard throughout the house. The man became spooked.

"What the fuck was that?" The man asked.

"I've no idea." Sarah-Jane replied. Before she could figure out what's going on, her door came open with a loud bang. A male police officer with 'Matthews' on his bulletproof vest came through the door.

"Ma'am, stop whatever you're doing. Face the wall and put your hands behind your back." The Police officer barked.

"What is going on?" Sarah-Jane demanded.

"Ma'am, face the wall and put your hands behind your back." Sarah-Jane did as she was told. The next thing she knew handcuffs were being put on her.

"You're under arrest for prostitution," Officer Matthews told her as he handcuffed her, "You have the right to remain silent. Anything you may say may be used as evidence which you may rely on in court." Sarah-Jane's heart began to race a mile a minute. Her cheeks blushed as she was dragged out of the room and into the hallway. She was made to sit with a few other girls who were in various stages of undress.

"Excuse me," Sarah-Jane piped up, "But couldn't have you let these girls get dressed before you arrested them?"

"Don't speak until spoken to or you'll end up in a police cell with your boss." At that moment, Sarah-Jane spotted Madame Beau being taken away in cuffs. It scared her enough to remain reluctantly quiet. Time passed slowly as each woman was processed individually by the police. A few moments later, Sarah-Jane was picked up and taken into the living room. Officer Matthews sat with a female police officer with "Cartwright" on her bulletproof vest.

"Can you tell me your name?" Officer Matthews asked.

"Sarah-Jane Weston."

"Date of birth."

"11th March 1999."

"Can you prove you have a right to work and live in the UK?" This question threw Sarah-Jane off.

"I was born and grew up in the UK. Why do you want to know?"

"Can you prove it?"

"My passport is at home."

"We'll have to have a look into it."

"Can't one of my friends just come and bring my passport? I only live next door"

"Miss, you're under arrest. You don't get to make demands."

"Matthews, go easy on the girl. She was asking a question." Officer Cartwright chimed. Officer Matthews glared briefly at Sarah-Jane.

"You're going to stay here until we get a hold of your passport and prove your right to live in the UK." Officer Matthews explained.

"Are you going to charge me?" Sarah-Jane asked. At that moment, Officer Matthews left the room. Officer Cartwright sat across from Sarah-Jane.

"We're going to check your record on our database. Provided you have no prior convictions, you'll almost certainly end up with a warning." Officer Cartwright explained.

"What was all that about my passport?"

"We were informed that illegal immigrants were working in this brothel. We have to check everyone's immigration status." A silence fell in the room. Officer Matthews came back into the room. He faced Officer Cartwright.

"She hasn't got any priors and she's a citizen."

"She's getting a warning."

"But Cartwright -"

"She's not got any prior convictions. I think a warning is adequate." At that, Officer Matthews stormed out of the door. Officer Cartwright uncuffed Sarah-Jane.

"Do you want me to get your clothes for you?" Officer Cartwright asked.

"Please." Sarah-Jane responded.

That evening Sarah-Jane relayed the story to Reuben, Kizzie and Diana.

"Shit me sideways." Reuben exclaimed.

"I was scared this would happen." Diana admitted, "I mean you see it on the news sometimes, but I didn't want to think it would happen to you."

"What are you going to do for a job?" Kizzie asked. At that minute, Diana's phone vibrated with a text message notification. She went to pick up her phone.

"Madame Beau still owes me some money from this week, but I doubt I'll see that," Sarah-Jane answered, "I'll just have to find another job and stretch the money I have."

"There might be a position going at my work," Reuben said, "I can have a word with my boss and see what I can do."

"You're a peach, Reuben." Sarah-Jane replied.

Suddenly Diana left the room. Everyone else noticed.

"Baby? What is it?" Kizzie shouted. She turned to look at Reuben and Sarah-Jane who were equally as perplexed as they heard Diana run up the stairs. They decided to follow after her. They reached the stairs and entered Diana & Kizzie's bedroom. Diana didn't register their entry.

"What's going on Diana?" Reuben asked. Diana furiously typed something into the computer. When the typing stopped, she saw something that made her stop in her tracks. She looked up at Sarah-Jane.

"What is it?" Sarah-Jane asked.

"Ehsan texted me to tell me. I didn't believe her but it's true." Diana said cryptically. Kizzie took the laptop from Diana to see what she meant. Her face

dropped as she turned to Sarah-Jane.

"SJ, Becky Matthews has somehow got a hold of the

footage from the raid this morning. She's -" Kizzie

started. She stopped when Reuben grabbed the laptop

away from Kizzie. His face dropped as he handed the

laptop to Sarah-Jane. Sarah-Jane scrolled through

what everyone else saw: an article detailing the raid

with Becky Matthew's blog as the source material.

Chapter Nine

Sarah-Jane handed the laptop back to Diana. She ran down the stairs back into the living room. She grabbed the remote control and turned the television on. Diana, Kizzie and Reuben rush down the stairs after her. Sarah-Jane watched her local news station as they reported on the raid.

"One of the women found in the raid has been identified as university student Sarah-Jane Weston. The bodycam footage mysteriously found its way to Conservative blogger Becky Matthews who editorialised Weston's involvement as an unsurprising moral failing. The university was contacted but has so far refused to comment." Those words echoed in Sarah-Jane's mind as she crumbled to the floor. Kizzie, Reuben and Diana gathered around her.

"SJ!" Reuben exclaimed.

"Kiz, get her some water." Diana ordered Kizzie who immediately did as she was told. Reuben and Diana helped Sarah-Jane up from her position onto the sofa. Kizzie returned with a glass of water. She held it out to Sarah-Jane, but she didn't take it.

"I think she's in shock." Diana commented.

"I'd be too if Becky cunting Matthews outed me like that." Reuben raged.

"How did she even get the footage? Scratch that," Kizzie wondered, "How did she know about the raid in the first place?"

"I think her brother works for the police or something," Diana answered, "Maybe that's how she got the footage."

"He needs to be punched in the fucking face, the scumbag." Reuben threatened.

"That's not helpful." Diana argued.

"I'm sorry but my best friend has been fucked over by Miss Holier Than Thou and the fucking police. Of course, I'm angry." Reuben explained.

"We need to think rationally here, or we'll end up screwing things further," Diana elucidated, "SJ will need to file a complaint with the Independent Police Complaints Commission." At that, Sarah-Jane suddenly got up. She grabbed the glass of water from Kizzie, drank it in one go and handed the glass back to Kizzie. She then left the room and ran to her bedroom, locking it behind her. Reuben, Kizzie and Diana stared at each other unsure what to do next.

Sarah-Jane refused to leave her bedroom the following day. She was dressed in her pyjamas and dressing gown, hair unbrushed and unkempt. She grabbed her mobile phone. She had a voicemail message waiting for her from her Mum. She decided to listen to it only to find Bob's voice speaking:

"Sarah-Jane Weston, this is your stepfather Bob speaking. Don't ever come back to this home. You're a fucking disgrace to the family. Your sister would be appalled if she were alive, you vile whore. Don't ever call us again."

Sarah-Jane paused for a moment as she processed the message in her head. She threw the phone across the room as she cried loudly. She crawled into her bed as she cried into her pillow. She felt like she would never stop crying as the memory of her dead sister came flooding back. She heard a soft knock on the door. She stopped crying. She looked at her door as the knocker tried to open the door.

"SJ, it's 3pm. You haven't eaten since yesterday. Can you open the door?" Reuben asked from behind the door. Sarah-Jane almost answered but stopped herself.

"SJ I can't imagine what you're going through, but you've got to eat. You can't punish yourself like this." Reuben pleaded.

"I'm not hungry," Sarah-Jane snapped. Regret hit her instantly for snapping at Reuben who was only trying to be kind.

"If you change your mind, I'll make you something to eat." Reuben answered before walking away. Sarah-Jane started hearing muttering from outside. She peaked slowly from behind her curtains to see some media camped outside her house. She retreated as quickly as she could. Her phone started ringing from her floor. She picked it up and answered it.

"Hello?"

"Ms Weston, this is the Dean of the University," The Dean answered, "I'm going to keep it brief. Due to your extracurricular activities, the university has decided to ban you from school grounds until a disciplinary hearing can take place. If you're found to be on school grounds you'll be expelled. Are we clear?"

"Crystal." Sarah-Jane croaked. She hung up the phone. She put the phone on her bedside table. She sat on her bed. She clutched the bed sheets as if her life depended on it. She stared down at the floor as she tried to process what was going on. She got lost in her thoughts until a loud knock sounded at her door. She stared at the door for a moment and tentatively decided to open the door. She opened it to find Luuk at her door with a suitcase. Sarah-Jane stepped back to let him in. He came in with his suitcase. He shut and locked the door behind him. They looked at each other before Sarah-Jane grabbed hold of Luuk and kissed him. Their embrace became passionate as they reached the bed. They continued to kiss intensely until Sarah-Jane reached for Luuk's trousers. He stopped kissing her.

"Are you sure?" He asked politely.

"I'm sure." Sarah-Jane replied. They undressed quickly until they were both naked. Luuk grabbed hold of Sarah-Jane. They fell into bed kissing each other. They reached for each other's private parts. Luuk started fingering Sarah-Jane whilst she stroked his penis. Luuk started kissing Sarah-Jane's neck as his fingering got faster. Sarah-Jane lost grasp of him as he pleasured her. She quickly came close to an orgasm when Luuk stopped. He grinned at her as he went for his trouser pocket to reveal a condom. He quickly placed it on his erect member. He went back to bed. Sarah-Jane pushed him on his back. She sat on him and placed him inside of her slowly. She started to rock up and down slowly. A wave of pleasure came over Sarah-Jane. Luuk held on to her hips as she got faster and faster with her movement. She moaned as she orgasmed on top of him. The more she came, the more she enjoyed herself. She panted in exhaustion as her hungry state hadn't left much energy. Luuk sensed this as he moved her off of him and on to her back. He inserted himself back inside of her. He tenderly went back and forth, rocking gently as he played with her clitoris. She felt another wave of pleasure start to build as he touched her. With one hand she clung to the bedsheets, with the other she dug her hand into his back. They continued to fuck each other until she was on the edge of another orgasm.

"Hold it," Luuk whispered. Understanding him, Sarah-Jane held on to her urge to orgasm whilst he continued to fuck her. After a moment, he started to orgasm.

"Now" he commanded. That was when they both experienced an orgasm in unison. They held each other tightly as their shared orgasm crashed through them. They looked into each other's eyes. Luuk got out of Sarah-Jane and headed into the bathroom. She joined him. He removed his condom, wrapped it in a toilet roll and put it in the bin. Sarah-Jane sat on the toilet.

"Hello." She jokingly greeted him.

"Hello there." He cheekily replied. He went over to Sarah-Jane and kissed her on the forehead. He went back into the bedroom and began getting dressed. Sarah-Jane briefly peed before clearing herself up.

"Who got you here?" she asked as she wiped herself.

"Kizzie. She still had my email from when you lost your phone during placement." Luuk replied as he pulled his underwear back on.

"How long are you here for?" Sarah-Jane asked as she pulled the flush. She washed her hands.

"A few days. I told work I had a family emergency." Luuk answered. Sarah-Jane smiled as she dried her hands. She walked back into the bedroom to find Luuk in his trousers. She sat on the bed. He sat next to her.

"Kizzie has just messaged me asking if we want any food. I've asked her to bring some ingredients so I can cook us something nice," Luuk told Sarah-Jane, "If I do this, are you going to eat?" Sarah-Jane reluctantly nodded.

"Good. Now get dressed," Luuk continued, "I don't expect you to go outside but I think we should get you out of this room."

Darkness fell across Flemington. Sarah-Jane sat in a jumper and jeans in the kitchen as Luuk cooked. It was the first time since the raid that she felt able to smile. At that moment Reuben came into the room. He spotted Sarah-Jane's smile.

"Now that's what I like to see." Reuben remarked as he sat next to Sarah-Jane. Kizzie entered the kitchen.

"I knew I smelt something good. What are you cooking, Luuk?" Kizzie asked. She sat next to Reuben.

"Stamppot," Luuk answered, "It's like Bubble & Squeak."

"It smells amazing." Kizzie keenly said.

"How're you feeling, sweetness?" Reuben asked Sarah-Jane. She turned to face Reuben.

"A little better but still pretty crappy. The university has banned me from campus until a disciplinary meeting can happen." Sarah-Jane responded.

"What about your work?" Kizzie asked.

"I imagine I'll have to email my lecturers and ask for my work to be sent to me," Sarah-Jane responded, "What was uni like for you two? Was anything said?" Reuben and Kizzie hesitated as Luuk finished cooking. He started placing the meal on two plates.

"SJ, do you want the truth or would you rather I didn't say anything?" Reuben enquired.

"The truth," Sarah-Jane resolved, "I need to know."

"There was a minor media circus outside the university. They made getting into uni a bit tricky." Kizzie admitted.

"I saw that bitch Becky Matthews trotting around like her shit didn't smell. It took every fibre of my being not to yell at her." Reuben continued.

"This Becky is the one who revealed Sarah-Jane's job?" Luuk asked as he placed his and Sarah-Jane's meals on the table. He sat next to Sarah-Jane.

"Yeah. She's this -" Reuben started.

"I know. Sarah-Jane already told me she's a righteous sort," Luuk interrupted, "I have a feeling there's more to this than meets the eye. Normal people don't go so out of the way to do this to someone they don't like."

"Becky is vicious in her righteousness," Kizzie noted, "But I see your point."

"We just have to figure out what's driving her to do this beyond her usual bitchy religious crap," Reuben continued, "Maybe she -" Reuben was interrupted by a knock at the door. He got up to go answer it whilst Sarah-Jane and Luuk ate. A minute later he came back with Diana and Ehsan.

"Ehsan," Sarah-Jane blurted, "What are you doing here?"

"We just got back from a meeting with the Feminist Society. We want to fight your corner." Ehsan replied.

Chapter Ten

"What?" Sarah-Jane asked, confused.

"I spoke to the Feminist Society about what happened to you," Diana confessed, "They're very keen to mobilise in your defence."

"They'll only do something if you're okay with it," Ehsan continued, "They don't want to violate your wishes."

"I'd consider it," Kizzie advised, "After all, what could you possibly lose?" Sarah-Jane hesitated. She looked around the room to see the empathetic faces of everyone around her. She looked down at her dinner.

"I don't deserve this." Sarah-Jane muttered.

"Yes you do," Reuben shrieked, "You've been fucked over by misogynistic forces that inexplicably still exist in our world."

"Think about it: you'd do the same if it was one of us," Diana retorted, "You'd be screaming bloody murder." Sarah-Jane half smiled. She sighed.

"Okay," she agreed, "I'm not allowed on school grounds so maybe we should meet here tomorrow?"

"Okay. I'll let the rest of the society know and get back to you." said Ehsan.

"Thanks folks." Sarah-Jane thanked everyone.

The following afternoon, Sarah-Jane and Luuk lay together in bed cuddled up to one another.

"Does the rest of the world need to exist right now?" Sarah-Jane asked coyly.

"I'm afraid it does," Luuk sadly confirmed, "It's terrible I know."

"If this notoriety doesn't die down then I may have to become a hermit." Sarah-Jane suggested jokingly.

"What if you wanted to come visit me in the Netherlands?" Luuk pointed out. Sarah-Jane smiled.

"Damn. I've been foiled once again," she jokingly proclaimed, "Perhaps I'll need to become a ninja to avoid detection."

"You don't own nunchucks," he pointed out.

"Do you ever turn off your lawyer brain?"

"Not especially. It's what makes me charming."

Sarah-Jane kissed Luuk on the lips. Suddenly Sarah-Jane's phone started ringing. She picked it up.

"Hello? Yes this is her . . . Hello. Yes. Yes I know . . . Okay. I'll be there. Thank you." Sarah-Jane hung up the phone. She turned back to Luuk.

"My university rang me," Sarah-Jane explained, "The disciplinary is tomorrow at 10:30am."

"Right. Do you want me to come with you?" Luuk asked.

"Nah. I should be okay. I've got to fight this one on my own." Sarah-Jane turned down. She kissed Luuk again.

"Thanks though." Sarah-Jane thanked him.

"It's okay." Luuk responded. They started to make out with each other until a knock was heard from the door.

"Are you decent? The Feminist Society will be around soon." Kizzie shouted through the door. Sarah-Jane looked longingly at Luuk. She grinned.

"When are they due?" Sarah-Jane shouted at Kizzie.

"Half an hour." Kizzie responded.

"I'll be ready by then." Sarah-Jane shouted back at Kizzie. She looked cheekily at Luuk.

"I'll get dressed in 25 minutes." Sarah-Jane teased. She was about to move when another knock boomed at the door.

"Luuk," Reuben said through the door, "Diana and I could use your help with something."

"Okay give me a minute." Luuk answered. Luuk looked longingly at Sarah-Jane.

"I think we're going to have to wait." Luuk resigned.

30 minutes later Kizzie and Sarah-Jane sat in their living room. A jug of water with plastic cups sat on the table. Sarah-Jane was clutching a share-size packet of crisps. Kizzie noticed Sarah-Jane's tension.

"How're you feeling?" Kizzie asked.

"Honestly? Scared," Sarah-Jane admitted, "I'm glad you're here."

"These are good people," Kizzie explained, "You'll be safe." The front door knocked. Kizzie got up and answered the door to Ehsan and a group of 6 people with name labels on their jackets. They held blank signs and sharpies in their hands.

"Thank goodness it's you," Kizzie sighed with relief, "I thought the press had returned."

"We're friendly I promise." Ehsan joked with Kizzie. Kizzie allowed them to come into the living room. She sat next to Sarah-Jane. Ehsan and two members of the Feminist Society sat on the sofa whilst the rest of the group sat on the floor. There was an awkward silence for a moment.

"Does anyone want any crisps?" Sarah-Jane asked.

"Why don't we put the crisps on the table then people can have some if they want some." Kizzie suggested.

"The crisps are very kind." A member called Chris piped up.

"Yeah we rarely have anything beyond water," A member called Stephanie added. Stephanie and Chris started pouring water for everyone in the room and handed water out.

"Team, let's cut to the chase. We all know what's happened to Sarah-Jane," A member called Bailey started, "We should work out what we need to do." The members of the Feminist Society all nodded in agreement.

"Sarah-Jane, is there anything you'd like?" Ehsan asked. Everyone turned to face Sarah-Jane. Sarah-Jane hesitated.

"What are you prepared to do?" Sarah-Jane asked.

"We can organise some protests." Ehsan suggested.

"Ooh I like the idea of a sit in." Stephanie gleefully contributed.

"I don't know, we need to catch the press attention," A member called Naomi pointed out.

"We can always send a press release for a sit-in," A member called Yasmine mentioned.

"How about a sit *out*? We could camp outside the campus and refuse to move," A member called Ali remarked, "A bit like the Occupy movement." The other members nodded.

"What do you think, SJ?" Ehsan asked. Everyone turned to Sarah-Jane.

"I like that idea. When would you start?" Sarah-Jane enquired.

"The press are still buzzing around the university during the day. We can start in the morning." Ehsan answered.

"I can get us a discount on tents from my job." Naomi chimed in.

"Wait, you're really going to do this for me?" Sarah-Jane said in disbelief.

"Of course." Ehsan replied.

"Why wouldn't we?" Stephanie added.

"Yeah this outing and the way you've been treated by the press has been a disgrace." Chris elaborated.

"We'd be a pretty shit bunch of feminists if we didn't step in to do something." Yasmine joined in. Sarah-Jane smiled at all of the Feminist Society members. She was genuinely touched by everything they were prepared to do.

"This means so much to me," Sarah-Jane said through a coy smile, "I don't know how to thank you all."

"There's no need," Ehsan assured her.

"How're you feeling?" Kizzie asked Sarah-Jane.

"Honestly a bit better," Sarah-Jane answered, "I feel better knowing I've got some more support." At that moment, Reuben stormed into the living room.

"You'll want to see this." Reuben told Kizzie and Sarah-Jane.

Chapter Eleven

"What is it, Reuben?" Kizzie asked.

"I'm not joking," Reuben responded, "You've got to see what we found." Reuben left the room. Intrigued, Kizzie and Sarah-Jane followed him into the kitchen. Luuk and Diana were gathered around Diana's laptop.

"What's going on?" Sarah-Jane enquired.

"Remember I had a feeling about Becky's motives?" Luuk started.

"Luuk was right on the money," Diana continued, "Becky has a secret."

"Which is?" Kizzie asked.

"She's a sex worker: doing the exact same thing SJ did." Reuben announced. Kizzie and Sarah-Jane's jaws dropped.

"Excuse me but what the fuck?" Sarah-Jane blurted.

"A sex worker this whole time?" Kizzie exclaimed.

"She uses that website DavesList to advertise herself under the pseudonym 'Rebecca Sweet Cheeks.'" Diana explained.

"The number listed on the site matches the one on her irritating Christian Conservative group flyers," Reuben continued, "It's her."

"It gets better: we didn't want to just believe the listing and leave it at that so between the three of us we contacted her via the listing using my picture." Luuk told the group.

"We said we'd pay her £10 for a sexy voicemail message and she didn't disappoint." Diana revealed, holding her phone in the air.

"We wanted to wait for you to be done before we listened to it." Reuben admitted.

"Let's hear it." Diana played her voicemail from Becky on loudspeaker:

"Hey baby, it's Rebecca Sweet Cheeks. I really want to touch your hot cock tonight. Let me know if you want to meet up hun, I want to blow your brains out. Rates start at £50." Sarah-Jane burst out laughing uncontrollably.

"The most prim and proper bitch of religious righteousness goes by the alias 'Rebecca Sweet Cheeks' to act as a sex worker yet has it in her to expose and shame me for doing the same thing,"

Sarah-Jane squealed, "Of course it's fucking funny."

"What do you want to do?" Luuk asked Sarah-Jane.

"I think you should expose that bitch the same way

she exposed you." Reuben chimed in enthusiastically.

"She's a total hypocrite. She deserves to go down."

Kizzie interjected.

"I know what she did is hypocritical, but I want to

meet with her first. I want to give her a chance to

retract her anti-sex tirade." Sarah-Jane decided.

"Does she really deserve that?" Diana asked.

"Yeah I mean she didn't exactly have compassion for

your position," Kizzie advised, "Plus she's a total

bitch."

"I know she lacks any compassion for anyone that isn't just like her but that doesn't mean I have to act the same way," Sarah-Jane maintained, "I doubt she'll meet me in person though."

"Diana, why don't you text her and pretend you're super into meeting her?" Reuben suggested. Before Diana could pick up her phone, she got a text message from Becky.

"Baby, if you want to meet you've got to snap me up quick! Meet me outside the University of Flemington and I'll show you a good time." Diana read out.

"That was a good coincidence." Luuk remarked.

"Bit pushy, isn't it?" Reuben pondered in a snarky tone.

"Maybe she's into who she *thinks* she's texting?" Kizzie suggested.

"I can see why," Sarah-Jane added. Luuk and Sarah-Jane shared a quick smile.

"I'll text her back and organise a meet up for tomorrow." Diana confirmed with the rest of the group.

"I'll get my printer so we can print all this stuff off." Kizzie said as she went to get her printer.

A few hours passed. Reuben, Kizzie and Diana were gathered in Kizzie & Diana's room waiting for things to print. Luuk and Sarah-Jane sat together on Sarah-Jane's bed. They sat in a near awkward silence.

"I'll say it," Luuk suddenly said as he faced Sarah-Jane, "I like you a lot. I think you're amazing. We have a lot of fun together." Luuk trailed off somewhat.

"But?" Sarah-Jane anticipated.

"There's no but," Luuk rebutted, "I like you."

"I like you too," Sarah-Jane replied, "Probably a little more than I should."

"That makes two of us." Luuk responded. They held hands.

"I don't know how it's going to work but would you be willing to give us a try?" Luuk asked.

"Would Zara be okay with that?" Sarah-Jane wondered.

"She figured this was coming. She's fine." Luuk assured her. Sarah-Jane smiled.

"In that case, let's give this a go." Sarah-Jane said as she continued to smile. They kissed each other which turned to them making out on the bed. They could barely get enough of each other. Sarah-Jane started kissing down Luuk's neck as she unbuttoned his shirt. She then started kissing down his bare chest until she reached his trousers. She unzipped his trousers and slid them and his underwear off of him. She looked upon his engorged member. She looked up at Luuk briefly before she started to lick the tip of his penis. Before they knew it, she had his penis in her mouth. She went up and down rhythmically with her mouth. As she continued, she reached for her clitoris and started to play with herself. She began to moan as she kept sucking him off. She would move herself up and down in rhythm with her playing with herself. Luuk eventually grabbed a hold of her hair, making her stop. Sarah-Jane moved her head away from his penis and faced him.

"I want to fuck you," He whispered, "Get on your knees." He let go of her hair. Sarah-Jane got on her hands and knees on the side of the bed. Luuk ruffled through his trouser pocket to find a condom. He ripped the wrapper off, slid the condom on his enlarged cock and proceeded to slip inside of her. She let out a gasp as the sensation of his entry hit her. The anticipation began to grow as he slid back and forth inside of her. She began to feel the ecstasy arise within her when he reached around to play with her throbbing clitoris. This started to throw her over the edge into a total eclipse of a sweet orgasm. She moaned as she got closer and closer to coming.

"I want you to come on me." Luuk commanded as he thrust harder into Sarah-Jane. She couldn't contain herself anymore: she came so hard she thought she'd never stop. The more he pushed and pulled away, the more he touched her clitoris and the more she orgasmed. She smiled as the weight of the orgasm swept through her entire body.

"Oh God that felt so good." Sarah-Jane exclaimed as Luuk kept going back and forth inside of her. Just when she felt she could barely take anymore, Sarah-Jane started feeling that sensation burn from within her again. She clutched the bedding as he stopped playing with her clitoris.

"I'm going to cum." He told her. At that, he began to climax from inside of Sarah-Jane. She felt pins and needles surge through her body as she came down from her aroused state. She panted into her bed as Luuk removed himself from her.

"Are you okay?" Luuk asked, concerned at her state.

"More of that." Sarah-Jane blurted. Realising she was spaced out, he helped her up to the ensuite. He sat her down on the toilet, proceeded to remove his condom and threw it away. Sarah-Jane started wiping herself down there and came back to life a little whilst Luuk washed himself.

"I came so damn hard." Sarah-Jane remarked.

"I could tell. When you're ready, we'll get you into bed." Luuk said. Sarah-Jane pulled the flush. Luuk helped her up as they went back into the bedroom.

Chapter Twelve

It was 10:45am. Kizzie and Reuben waited outside the university with the protesting Feminist Society. They were holding placards that said things such as "Justice 4 Sarah-Jane" and "Sex work is legit." The wind picked up in the air as they waited at the door. A long pause hung in the atmosphere. Sarah-Jane came through the door. Her expression was washed out and exhausted.

"Well?" Kizzie asked kindly. Sarah-Jane looked at Kizzie then at Reuben then at the Feminist Society who hung on her every word.

"They're keeping me in the university. I'm on probation but I'm still on the course!" Sarah-Jane announced. The Feminist Society all rose up in applause.

"Fuck yes SJ," Reuben hurrahed. He gave Sarah-Jane a huge hug.

"I'm so pleased," Kizzie cheered as she gave Sarah-Jane a hug.

"I'm so relieved," Sarah-Jane sighed, "It's a shame Luuk and Diana couldn't be here."

"Why don't we all go to the pub?" Reuben suggested.

"We've got The Thing to do later today," Sarah-Jane cryptically reminded Reuben, "But maybe a drink at home would be fun?"

"Everyone: drinks at our place from 8pm!" Kizzie yelled. Everyone cheered. The Feminist Society started to pack away their tents.

"I've got a lecture to go to, but I love you and you're amazing," Reuben hurriedly told Sarah-Jane as he ran into the university building. Kizzie & Sarah-Jane linked arms and started walking away from the university.

"I wish this was over," Sarah-Jane mused, "But I get the impression it might never be."

"What makes you say that?" Kizzie asked.

"This sort of thing sticks," Sarah-Jane replied, "I mean it's not like Christine Keeler got to live a normal life even after the Profumo scandal died down."

"You didn't fuck Russian spies or the Secretary of War." Kizzie pointed out.

"True but there's not a lot of distinction in the eyes of the public."

"Eyes of the public or eyes of your dickhead stepdad?"

"Both?"

"Has your Mum even spoken to you?"

"She left a message whilst I was with Luuk last night. I'm not hopeful."

"I know you're bound to still feel burnt by this whole experience but try to hang on to the good things: you're still on your course, you've got a supportive boyfriend and friends who adore you."

"Thanks."

6pm struck. Becky Matthews was sitting on her table expectantly. She tapped her fingers as she waited for company. The door knocked.

"Come in," she invited. She stood up. She looked at the door happily. Her face dropped when she saw

Sarah-Jane walk through the door with a pile of paper in her hand.

"I'm appalled you feel you can show your whore face." Becky spat at her. Sarah-Jane smiled at her which threw Becky off.

"What are you doing?" Becky asked in a demanding fashion.

"You're fucking hilarious." Sarah-Jane answered, trying not to laugh.

"What?" Becky spewed.

"You go around preaching bigoted nonsense in the name of your religion. You shamed me for being a sex worker and yet you're just as much a sex worker as me!" Sarah-Jane revealed.

"What?!" Becky sputtered, trying to mask her shock.

"You thought you were meeting a hot Dutch man called Luuk. Too bad: you fell for a picture of my boyfriend and were texting Diana the whole time," Sarah-Jane continued, "Don't believe me? Here." Sarah-Jane handed the pile of paper to Becky who proceeded to rip it up.

"Ha! There! No one will believe you now," Becky spat at Sarah-Jane as she threw the pieces in the air, "No one would believe a dirty whore." Sarah-Jane folded her arms.

"Do you have any idea what you've done to my life?" Sarah-Jane asked.

"Not enough, obviously." Becky snorted.

"You ruined my relationship with my family. You almost got me kicked out of university and you may have ruined my chances of getting a career I've worked my arse off to obtain. I know you don't like me, and I hardly like you, but you had no right to do what you did to me."

"You're a sinner in the eyes of the Lord. I pledged my heart to the Almighty Father. This world is infested with heathens like you who need to be punished."

"You're a Goddamn hypocrite! You tried to ruin my whole life by exposing me as a sex worker whilst working as a sex worker yourself. No amount of pontification gets rid of that."

"Fine! I'm a whore. I love to fornicate for money. Are you happy now?" Becky screamed at Sarah-Jane. Becky stepped back.

"You don't have to be like this Becky," Sarah-Jane advised, "You don't have to be this all high and mighty pain in the arse. You can still believe in God. It -"

"I'm not interested in being like you, you damn sinner." Becky viciously interrupted. Becky stormed off, slamming the door behind her. Sarah-Jane reached into her pocket to reveal her phone with its voice recorder on. She placed the phone by her mouth.

"I'm sorry," Sarah-Jane remarked, "But you won't learn otherwise." She turned off the phone's recording feature.

Two hours after Sarah-Jane returned home, defeated. She shut the door behind her. She went into the living room where Reuben, Diana and Kizzie were waiting for her.

"What happened?" Reuben asked. Sarah-Jane took her phone out of her pocket. She placed the phone on the coffee table. She played the recording. Reuben, Diana and Kizzie listened intently. As it played, Sarah-Jane sat on the sofa and put her head in her hands. She sighed as the recording ended.

"I don't know what you were expecting to be honest." Diana pointed out.

"She is an unbearable crank." Kizzie remarked.

"Reuben, can you transfer the recording onto your laptop?" Sarah-Jane asked.

"Sure. I'll get on it." Reuben took Sarah-Jane's phone and went upstairs.

"How're you feeling?" Kizzie asked Sarah-Jane.

"Exhausted. I really hoped I could've helped her."
Sarah-Jane answered.

"Some people are beyond help. You can't solve everything." Diana remarked.

"I know," said Sarah-Jane.

"We can contact the university tomorrow with what we've got." Kizzie told her.

"It feels a bit short to only go to the university with this." Diana pondered. At that moment, a knock on the door sounded. Sarah-Jane answered the door to Ehsan, Stephanie and Chris from the Feminist Society. They had their laptops in their hands.

"Are you ready for tomorrow?" Ehsan asked.

Chapter Thirteen

"What?" Sarah-Jane asked as she let Stephanie, Chris and Ehsan into the living room.

"Did Diana not tell you?" Stephanie asked as she sat on the sofa and started setting up her laptop. Chris sat next to her. Ehsan put her arm around Sarah-Jane.

"Diana?" Ehsan asked.

"I was *just* about to tell her." Diana explained.

"Tell me what?" Sarah-Jane inquired. Diana stood up.

"We're organising a Feminist Society press conference for tomorrow at 1pm," Diana explained.

"This is the perfect avenue to out Becky." Reuben interjected.

"Out her?" Ehsan asked, confused. Everyone faced Sarah-Jane. She was still a little conflicted but pushed forward.

"Okay. There's something you should know about Becky Matthews."

The next day dawned on the residents of Flemington, but Sarah-Jane had barely slept. Still in the clothes she wore the day before, she continued to stare at the ceiling until her alarm went off, signalling it was 10am. She allowed the alarm to blare for a few seconds before turning it off. A few more seconds passed. She realised she was horny and wanted to masturbate. Before she could make a meaningful decision, a knock was heard at her bedroom door.

"SJ, have you had breakfast yet? You need to get ready for the press conference." Reuben shouted from the other side of the door. Sarah-Jane didn't respond for a moment. She looked to the door and started to move off the bed.

"No. I just need to shower," Sarah-Jane replied, "Give me a few minutes."

"Okay" Reuben shouted as he walked away. Sarah-Jane stripped out of her clothes, chucked them in her washing basket then trotted to the shower. She reached into her underwear drawer and withdrew a waterproof bullet vibrator. She went into her ensuite, turned on the shower and jumped in. The warm water splashed upon her as she started to tease her clitoris. She moaned as she started thinking about wanting to have sex with someone she doesn't know.

As she quietly moaned and enjoyed herself with one hand, she inserted the waterproof bullet vibrator into her vagina. As she started manoeuvring her vibrator back and forth, Sarah-Jane started to orgasm. She stopped teasing her clitoris and moved that hand to the side of the shower. She couldn't help but give out a gasp of pleasure as her orgasm waved over her. As she came down from the intense pleasure, Sarah-Jane placed her vibrator on her sink shelf. She jumped back into the shower to wash herself properly.

1pm rolled around. The usually uneventful university theatre lecture space was full of students, faculty and members of the press armed with cameras and microphones. The members of the Feminist Society sat in seats behind the lectern armed with stacks of paper. A laptop was sitting near the lectern on a seat. A screen stood behind the lectern. In a side room next to the theatre, Sarah-Jane and Kizzie were preparing.

"Are you ready?" Kizzie asked. Sarah-Jane sighed.

"I've got to be. I'm here now." Sarah-Jane replied. Reuben came through the door. He put his arms around Kizzie and Sarah-Jane.

"It's time," Reuben started, "Diana is ready to assume security position with you Kizzie in case Becky tries to stop everything."

"Perfect. I'll see you after it's all done," Kizzie said as she left to join Diana in the lecture room entrance. Reuben hugged Sarah-Jane.

"You've got this," Reuben reassured her as he broke away from her, "Shall we go together?" Sarah-Jane nodded. They walked into the university lecture hall together. Reuben went to the laptop and set up the presentation as Sarah-Jane approached the lectern. At that, cameras started taking pictures whilst others began filming. A pitter patter of chatter spread across the room. Sarah-Jane looked to Reuben, looked at the Feminist Society then looked at the audience. She cleared her throat.

"Good afternoon. I appreciate you all being here," Sarah-Jane paused, thinking about what she was going to say, "I know you've all seen the news reports of my extracurricular activities." Sarah-Jane paused again. She looked at Kizzie and Diana who gave her a thumbs up. She looked back at the audience.

"I would like to start with this: sex work should be legitimate work, but we seem to, time and time again, fail to make this a reality. The fact is that whilst human sex trafficking absolutely exists and needs to be stopped, there are people out there who want to do sex work as a real way of life whether they want to do what I did or pursue other forms of sex work. We shouldn't be demonising people like me. We should be challenging the patriarchal constructs that allow the stigma to continue. The truth is, I enjoyed what I did, and I don't feel like I have to justify myself to anyone." Sarah-Jane stopped to look at the audience. A few of the members started to clap. Sarah-Jane felt a surge of confidence she hadn't felt for a while.

"But this isn't just a declaration in favour of pro-sex work legislation. This is about authenticity. This is about the conviction of one's beliefs. I would like the Feminist Society to now hand the papers to the members of the press." Sarah-Jane stepped back as the Feminist society handed out the papers to the members of the press. They quickly sat back down at their seats with one of the members handing a bundle of papers to Sarah-Jane. She went back to the lectern.

"Reuben, can you head to the first slide?" Sarah-Jane requested. Reuben did as he was asked. At that moment, Becky came thundering into the lecture room but was stopped by Diana and Kizzie. Sarah-Jane spotted her. She was temporarily phased but she kept going.

"Now you can see here a text exchange between a gentleman called Luuk and what appears to be a lady going by the name of Rebecca Sweet Cheeks. I can reveal exactly who it was. Reuben, next slide." A slide appeared on the screen behind Sarah-Jane that simply showed an audio file. A look of panic spread across Becky's face. This was quickly eclipsed by anger.

"It's not real," Becky began to scream as she tried to get past Kizzie and Diana, "It's fake!" Sarah-Jane faced Becky with a smile.

"Hit it, Reuben!" Sarah-Jane commanded. Reuben pressed play. The sexy voicemail message left on Diane's phone played. It was undeniable for all in the room. As the audio played, Becky stood in astonishment.

"That's not all folks," Sarah-Jane continued as the audio ended, "I was very conflicted about doing this. I wanted to give Becky Matthews a chance to take down her posts and be done with it, but she was so set in her ways she didn't seem to think anyone could take her down. Next slide, Reuben." Reuben went to the next slide that contained another audio file. Becky, now incandescent with rage, tried once more to get past Diana and Kizzie. Reuben played the audio of Sarah-Jane's last conversation with Becky. As the audio ended, cameras started turning to Becky.

"I gave you a chance, Becky. You ruined my life with glee. Everyone can see your hypocrisy for what it really is. Enjoy reaping what you sowed." Becky, realising the cameras were on her, ran away.

"I would take questions, but I think you got what you need. This press conference is done." Sarah-Jane walked away, satisfied she'd done what she needed to do.

Epilogue

It was six months later. Spring was turning into summer over the coastal town of Flemington. A congregation of graduate students with their families were outside in the courtyard of the University of Flemington. The graduates were a sea of black graduation robes and mortarboards. Among them was Sarah-Jane. She stood alone, watching other people celebrate with their families. She got out her phone to see a text from Luuk. She sighed. She contemplated leaving when she heard:

"Sarah-Jane!" She turned to see Diana, Reuben and Kizzie. She went to them.

"I thought you folks would be with your families?" Sarah-Jane asked.

"Mine and Diana's are currently doing the awkward "Get to know the in-laws" bit." Kizzie answered.

"Mine have already left," Reuben contributed, "Did yours not come?"

"No," Sarah-Jane answered awkwardly, "And I wouldn't want them there anyway. Mum chose Stepdad over me. She can live with the consequences." An uncomfortable silence fell among the foursome. Sarah-Jane decided to quickly change the subject:

"I know we still technically live together but I'm so glad to see you." Sarah-Jane said as she brought them in for a group hug. They broke apart.

"What are you going to do now, SJ?" Diana asked.

"I'm away next week to spend a month with Luuk in the Netherlands. I think I just need a break from things here. Everything was so crazy." Sarah-Jane replied.

"It was just crazy being near it," Kizzie chimed in, "Hopefully the break will do you some good."

"I'll miss you all," Sarah-Jane said as she fought back tears, "Promise you'll keep in touch with me."

"Wouldn't want it any other way," Reuben said as he held Sarah-Jane.

"We better get back to our families," Diana lamented, "We'll see you at home?"

"Sure" Sarah-Jane nodded. Diana and Kizzie left. Sarah-Jane turned to Reuben.

"Fancy a drink? I feel the need to decompress this year through major alcohol consumption." Sarah-Jane proposed to Reuben. He smiled.

"Fuck yes, SJ." He agreed. They walked away together arm-in-arm, leaving the mass of graduates to their celebrations.

ACKNOWLEDGEMENTS

With thanks to the person who inspired the story, the initial readers of the story who kept me in check, my editor for her enthusiasm and everyone who read this book. It all means more than words can truly express.